My little fish

My little fish is

beside the rock.

My little fish is

beside the boat.

My little fish is

beside the plant.

My little fish is

beside the shell.

My little fish is

beside the diver.

My little fish is

beside the cave.

My little fish is ...

inside the cave.